The Little Mermaid

STERLING CHILDREN'S BOOKS
New York

TEXT ADAPTATION GIADA FRANCIA • GRAPHIC DESIGN MARINELLA DEBERNARDI

BASED ON A FAIRY TALE BY
Hans Christian Andersen

ILLUSTRATIONS BY
Francesca Rossi

In the middle of the ocean, where the water is as clear as the purest crystal, there lies a magical kingdom. You mustn't think there's only sand and seaweed at the bottom of the ocean! For in its depths grow strange plants with stems and petals so fine that they swish at the slightest ripple in the water. All the fish, large and small, swim among the branches, just as birds do in the air. And once, long ago, there stood a magnificent palace.

The walls were made of coral, and the tall arched windows were of clear amber. The roof was formed by shells that opened and closed with the movement of the water. Each shell contained a marvelous pearl, worthy of a queen's crown.

In the castle lived the king of the sea. He had been a widower for many years, and his elderly mother ran the palace with wisdom and joy. She took care of the little princesses of the sea, her grandchildren, whom she loved very much.

They were seven lovely mermaids, charming creatures whose bodies ended in a fishtail. All day the princesses played in the palace gardens. Fish swam around them and ate from their hands, allowing themselves to be petted. Each mermaid had a little patch in the garden, where she could plant anything she wanted. One of the princesses grew her garden into the shape of a whale; another fashioned an octopus from the underwater blooms. But the youngest, littlest mermaid set up a marble statue of a handsome young man. She had found it sunken on the ocean floor after a shipwreck and decorated it with red flowers.

The little mermaid loved more than anything else to make up conversations with the statue. She spent lazy days imagining that the statue's face would come to life to describe his world—the world of humans. No other topic interested her more, and every night she begged her grandmother to tell her all she knew of ships and cities, humans and land animals.

"When you are eighteen," the grandmother said to the girls one evening, "you will be allowed to go to the surface. You can sit in the moonlight on the rocks and see so many things! It is a priceless gift."

The next month, the oldest princess celebrated her eighteenth birthday. But the little mermaid had to wait another five years before she could go to the surface. Her sisters promised to describe everything they saw during their first journey. None of them, however, was as curious as the little mermaid. For many nights she lingered at her window, gazing upward. She could glimpse the moon and the stars through the water. And if a black shadow blocked them out, she knew that maybe a ship with lots of people onboard had passed overhead. People, she sighed, who did not even know she existed.

When the oldest princess returned home after having observed the world on dry land, she described how nice it had been to lie in the moonlight on a sandbank in the middle of the calm sea. She had watched the big cities on the coast full of lights that twinkled like hundreds of stars.

The second sister, the bravest of them all, swam up a wide river that flowed into the sea. She saw rolling green hills with vineyards, castles, and farms. In a small cove, she met a dog, an animal that no mermaid had ever seen before. When it started to bark at her, she swam back to the open sea in terror. But she could never forget those wonderful woods and the green hills.

The third sister's birthday fell in the winter, when large magnificent icebergs floated all around.

The fourth sister was not so adventurous. She stayed in the middle of the open sea, but said it was heavenly nonetheless. At the surface she could look for miles in every direction at the sea and the sky, which seemed to merge at the horizon. She had seen ships, but from afar. The playful dolphins did somersaults in the air and great whales spouted water from their blowholes.

Then it was the fifth sister's turn. She looked out among the waves just as the sun was setting, and the sight left her speechless. The whole sky was golden; the clouds were purple and red. It was unlike anything she had seen.

The sixth sister more than anything else remembered the majesty of a flock of wild swans, who had flown overhead toward the sun.

The first time the mermaids left the water, they were all astonished by the new and wonderful things they saw. But once they had permission to go up whenever they wished, they stopped marveling at the wonders of the human world and began to appreciate more and more the depths of the sea. Every now and then, though, they would go to the surface together, arm in arm. There, the mermaids sang with voices so beautiful that they were capable of enchanting humans. Whenever there was a storm, the sisters swam to the ships that were about to capsize, and sang softly to the sailors so they would not be afraid.

On these occasions the little mermaid was left all alone in the castle, wanting more than anything to grow up quickly. When at last came the day of her long-awaited eighteenth birthday, her grandmother gave her a hug and placed a wreath of seaweed in her hair, then a garland of anemones around her neck. Then she attached eight large oysters to the princess's tail as a symbol of her nobility.

"Ouch!" muttered the princess. "That hurts!"

"My little one, I am certainly not going to let you go to the surface dressed like any old fish!" said her grandmother, attaching another shell.

The princess stopped complaining. She did not want to be late—not that day. When she was finally ready, the little mermaid took a deep breath. She waved to her sisters then began to swim firmly to the surface, rising as lightly as a bubble of air through the water. When her head popped out of the water, the sun was setting over the waves.

As the sun set and darkness fell, a large ship passed, and she heard music and songs. The little mermaid swam up to a porthole and stretched to peek through the glass. She saw that there was a party being held for a young prince. Like her, he was becoming an adult that day.

She was still enjoying watching the party when she heard the unmistakable roar of a storm in the distance. In a few moments the waves grew larger. Dark and threatening clouds appeared, and a very strong wind rose. Suddenly the ship was lifted up by the storm and creaked horribly, before collapsing and falling into the sea. The mast broke and the ship keeled over as it began to take on water.

The little mermaid realized the men on board were in danger. She looked for the prince and saw him sinking into the depths of the sea. The mermaid swam as fast as she could among the wreckage of the ship, plunging in and out of the waves until she reached the unconscious prince. She held his head up out of the water and allowed the tide to carry them out.

In the morning, after the storm had passed, there was no trace of the ship. But the sun rose and shone on the water. Its light touched the face of the prince, whose eyes were still shut. The little mermaid kissed him on the forehead and pushed back his wet hair. She looked at him for a long time, trying to remember where she had seen him before. Finally, she recalled the marble statue she had in her garden. The young man looked very similar! The little mermaid kissed him again, wanting desperately to save him. Then she saw the coast come into view.

At the top of a cliff she saw a house, or perhaps a church—the mermaid did not know the difference. But it was a large building, one that certainly had people in it. Oranges and lemons grew in the garden and a large staircase led down to a small beach where the sand was white and soft. She swam there with her handsome prince and laid him out on the sand, taking care to ensure that his head was raised and facing the warm sun.

When she saw people leaving the building, she hid
behind some high rocks and covered herself in sea foam so
that no one would see her. When she felt safe, she sang a
sweet song to attract the attention of the passers-by to the
sleeping young man. That enchanting voice was the first
thing that the prince heard when he woke up.

Sitting up, he looked around and smiled. But when he realized that there was no young girl in the crowd around him, he felt sad and wondered if he had only dreamed that sweet melody. The little mermaid saw the prince being helped away by a loyal subject, and she too was suddenly overcome by a great sadness. She dived into the water and returned to her father's castle. As soon as she entered the underwater palace, her sisters asked her what she had seen during her first outing. She did not tell them anything.

After that day she went back many times to the beach where she had left the prince, but never saw him. Each time, she returned home feeling more and more sad. Her only consolation was to go into her little garden and embrace the beautiful marble statue that looked so like him. After months of this, her concerned sisters begged her to tell them the reason why she was so sad. Deciding it was foolish to continue to keep her secret, she told them every detail of her first trip to the surface.

"Do not say a word to anyone, I beg you," she said. "Especially not to our father."

"Don't worry, little one," said her oldest sister. "We know that he would be furious if he found out that you loved a human. We won't tell him anything. But maybe I can help you. I think I know where to find your prince! Come, I'll take you to his palace so you can see him one last time, say good-bye, and start smiling again."

The mermaid took her little sister's hand and they swam toward the surface. When they arrived at the royal palace by the sea, the little mermaid gasped. She had never seen such a vast building! It was made of shiny yellow stone, and it had large marble staircases, one of which went down to the sea. Splendid golden domes rose up from the roof, and between the columns that surrounded the whole building stood marble statues. Through the glass of the tall windows she could see into wonderful large rooms with precious silk curtains and rugs, and large paintings on the walls.

Now that the little mermaid knew where the prince lived, she started sneaking away in the mornings and returning there often, getting closer and closer to the palace. She swam very close to the shore, as no mermaid had ever dared to do before. She gradually plucked up her courage and even went up the narrow channel that surrounded the castle, all the way to the magnificent marble terrace that cast a large shadow on the water. There she spent hours watching the young prince, who believed he was alone in the moonlight. She saw him many times sailing in a beautiful boat. Often she heard the fishermen, who spent the night on boats lit by lanterns, speak very well of him.

After a few weeks, the little mermaid no longer feared those whom her father called "fish-eaters." She learned to appreciate humans more and more each day, even wishing she could live among them.

There was so much of their world she wanted to know about. But one thought, more than anything, had stayed with her since she saved the prince. She asked her sisters but they were unable to answer her, so she decided to speak with her grandmother. Grandma knew a lot about "the land above the sea," as she called the world above.

"Grandma, there's one thing I want to know," she asked. "If you save a drowning man and take him back to land . . . will he live forever?"

"No, dear. Men die, too," said the old mermaid. "But unlike us, who turn into sea foam, men possess a soul that continues to live, and rises up through the air to the shining stars! Just as we climb up through the sea and see the land of people, so they rise up to beautiful unknown places that we can never see!"

"Why do we not have an immortal soul as well?" asked the little mermaid very sadly. "I'd give a hundred of the years that I still have to live like a human for just one day!"

"You cannot think such things!" boomed her father's voice behind her. "We are much happier, and we're certainly better than humans. My little one, you have to stop daydreaming about the world of men! You idealize them too much, but those silly fish-eaters would never welcome you!"

He shook his head and continued. "The thing that is so beautiful here, the fishtail, is considered horrible on land. For them, beauty lies in those strange supports they call legs and feet."

The little mermaid looked down at her fishtail and sighed.

"Now give me a nice smile and be happy, my child! Tonight is the palace ball." The sea king took his youngest daughter's hand. "The great hall has been beautifully decorated! Nothing that you might find up there could ever be better than the palace tonight."

He was not exaggerating. The throne room was a wonder, the likes of which had never been seen on land. Thousands of huge shells, pink and green, were lined up on each side. Countless fish, great and small, could be seen swimming beyond the glass walls.

In the middle of the room danced colorful jellyfish and crabs, while mermaids sang sweetly. The little mermaid felt happy at the ball, but soon enough her thoughts returned to the world on the surface, and the handsome prince she could not forget. She slipped quietly out of the castle and sat among the anemones, thinking that she would never give up the love she felt for the prince, not even for all the wonders of the underwater world.

"I know what I'll do!" she said decisively. "I'll go to the witch of the sea. I've always been scared of her, but she's the only one who can help me."

The little mermaid left her garden and set off for the cave where the witch lived. She had never traveled that path before. No coral grew there and the sand was gray. The water formed whirlpools that swallowed everything they could. Beyond these terrifying whirlpools was the witch's cave, guarded by eels and octopuses, who wrapped themselves around anything they could grab.

The little mermaid was terrified. Her heart pounded with fear. She was about to go back, but the thought of the prince gave her courage. She tied back her long hair so the octopuses could not grab hold of it, then darted like a fish past the horrible creatures. Before long she appeared in front of the sea witch, who seemed to be expecting her.

"I know what you want," the witch rasped. "To get rid of your fishtail so that the young prince will fall in love with you. Well, I can make you a potion. You must go up onto the beach and drink it before the sun rises. Then your tail will split in two and become what men call 'legs.' But once you've been transformed into a woman, you can never go back to being a mermaid! And if you do not win the love of the prince, you will be alone on land with no voice."

"No voice?" asked the mermaid, turning pale.

"Of course! You need to pay me, and my price is high. You have the most beautiful voice in the sea, and I want it for myself. Give me your voice as payment."

"All right," the mermaid said quietly.

The witch smiled and raised her hand, placing it on the princess's head. Out of the mermaid's mouth came a pearl, which the witch caught and placed in a shell.

"Take the potion and go. Good luck," said the witch, laughing.

The princess passed quickly through the swamp of octopuses and saw her father's castle in the distance. All the lights were turned off in the great ballroom.

Everyone was bound to be asleep, and she would not have dared look for them anyway. If they knew what she was doing they would certainly stop her. As she turned and swam to the surface, she felt as if her heart would break with the pain.

The sun had not yet risen when the little mermaid reached the beach. She took a final look at her long shiny tail, then drank the fiery potion. Immediately she felt a powerful heat in her body, so intense that she fainted.

When the sun rose on the horizon, she woke up to see the young prince staring at her, his eyes filled with concern. She looked down and saw that her fishtail was gone. She now possessed the most beautiful legs any girl had ever had!

The prince asked her who she was and how she had gotten there. She looked at him sweetly, but was unable to say a single word—her voice was trapped in the witch's shell. The prince helped her up, and for the first time she tried to walk like a human being on those weird fins called "feet."

The prince brought her into the palace, where she was made welcome. As a guest of His Majesty, she was treated as a visitor of high rank and was able to sit at the royal table during the banquet that evening. For the occasion, pretty maids sang before the prince and his parents. One of them sang better than the others, and the king turned to the prince.

"Is she the girl you're looking for?" the king asked.

But the prince shook his head and sighed. He rose from the table to go out into the garden. The little mermaid followed him.

"That must have seemed like a strange scene to you," the prince said when she caught up with him. "It has been repeated every evening for months. My father invites the most beautiful ladies of the kingdom and asks them to sing. It has been happening since the day my ship sank during the storm. When I woke up I heard a girl singing next to me. She had a really sweet voice; I will never forget it. I . . . I think I'm in love with her. You're smiling because you think this is foolish? You're right; I never even saw her."

But she did not find the prince's words foolish. They were exactly what she had dreamed of him saying ever since she left him on the beach. The little mermaid tried to explain to him, but she was unable to make a single sound. If only she could sing, then he would have recognized her!

"Now I've lost hope," he continued. "I'll never find the girl of my dreams, so I'll just have to accept the bride chosen for me by my parents."

The little mermaid looked at him in horror. She could not allow this to happen! Not after giving up her whole world for him.

"Are you all right?" he asked. "Maybe we should go back inside. Do you like dancing?"

She forced a smile and let him lead her into the ballroom, determined to have fun at least for that night—even if she did not know how to dance without a tail!

In the ballroom, the orchestra started to play and all the guests began to dance. The little mermaid watched them for a moment, then held out her arms toward the prince. She stood up on her toes and whirled, dancing with the grace of a mermaid, like no one had ever done before at the palace. Everyone was enchanted, especially the prince. After that evening, he did not want to be apart from her.

Together they rode through the woods where the green boughs brushed against their shoulders, and the little birds sang among the leaves. The little mermaid climbed with the prince in the high mountains, to where they could see the clouds below them moving as if they were flocks of birds traveling to foreign lands.

It was the life she had most desired, but at night the little mermaid would sneak out of the castle. She went to the beach and soothed her sore feet by placing them in the cool water, thinking of her family and all she had left behind.

One day, the prince had news for the little mermaid.

"I have to leave. I am to meet my future wife," he said. Noticing her shocked expression, he added, "I don't want to leave you, either! Come with me on this journey. You're not afraid of going by sea, are you?"

She smiled at these words, agreeing to join him. That evening, the two of them waited on the deck of the ship.

"My father has planned this wedding for months. He agreed to wait until I found the girl whose voice I keep dreaming about. But I understand now that I can see her only in my dreams. And since I met you I cannot help but imagine her with your face. If I could choose who to marry . . ."

He placed a kiss on her lips. Then, after looking sadly at her one more time, he went below decks.

As night fell, the little mermaid's sisters came up to the surface and approached the ship.

"Little sister, come home!" they begged. "Our father is in despair. He doesn't know where you are."

The little mermaid shook her head with her eyes full of tears.

"So you love him that much, then?" asked her oldest sister.

She nodded vigorously. There was no other way to explain to her sisters what she had felt when the prince

held her close to him. Even if she was not able to prevent the marriage that would end all her hopes, she felt she had to remain on land. She waved good-bye to the mermaids.

"There's only one thing to be done," said the oldest sister.

The princesses swam quickly to the underwater palace, found their father, and explained everything. The king of the sea was furious at first, but when he heard about the love that bound his youngest daughter to the human, he resigned himself.

"If that is what she wants to do, and if it makes her truly happy, then I will accept her decision," he said with a sigh.

"Father, that is not all. She no longer has her voice! The sea witch took it from her in exchange for the spell that turned her into a human!"

"What?" thundered the king. "How dare that old hag put her hands on my daughter!"

Enraged, he grabbed his trident and swam quickly to the witch's cave. His arrival was announced by the sentry eels, so the witch was prepared to face the king of the sea. With a spell she turned herself into a horrible giant octopus. She pounced on the king and ripped the trident from his hand.

The battle that followed was terrible. For many centuries the two old enemies had known that one day they would clash. That time had finally come. The witch clung to the king with her tentacles and began to crush him. But he summoned his army of dolphins and whales, who leaped on the witch and ripped her tentacles off.

Knowing she was defeated, the witch offered the shell with the little mermaid's voice in exchange for her life.

The king had her locked up in a coral prison. Then, with the shell in his hand, he went up to the surface, emerging among the waves in front of the prince's ship. He saw his daughter on the deck staring sadly at the horizon and felt all his anger vanish. He knew what to do to give her back her smile.

"My girl, if this is the life you really desire, you have my approval," said the sea king, offering his astonished daughter the pearl that contained her voice.

Weeping, she swallowed the pearl, then said, "I love you, Father!"

The little mermaid closed her eyes and began to sing the same sweet song she had sung to the prince when she rescued him. When she finished, she opened her eyes and saw the young man standing next to her.

"You! You're the girl of my dreams! I . . . I knew it," whispered the prince.

He took her in his arms and promised to never let her go.

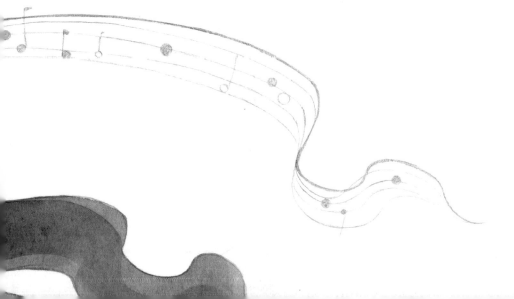

STERLING CHILDREN'S BOOKS
New York

An Imprint of Sterling Publishing
387 Park Avenue South
New York, NY 10016

First Sterling edition 2015
First published in Italy in 2014 by De Agostini Libri S.p.A.

ISBN 978-1-4549-1509-6

Distributed in Canada by Sterling Publishing
c/o Canadian Manda Group, 165 Dufferin Street
Toronto, Ontario, Canada M6K 3H6
For information about custom editions, special sales, and premium and
corporate purchases,
please contact Sterling Special Sales at 800-805-5489
or specialsales@sterlingpublishing.com.

Translation: Contextus s.r.l., Pavia, Italy (Louise Bostock)
Editor: Contextus s.r.l., Pavia, Italy (Martin Maguire)

Manufactured in China
Lot #:
2 4 6 8 10 9 7 5 3 1
11/14
www.sterlingpublishing.com/kids